One 'n Done #5

The Legend of Dave Bradley

A performance piece by
S Atzeni

Published by

Read Often. Read Well.
Read Furiously

But first...

The following is a true story.

The following story is mostly true.

The following story is partially true, told to anyone who will still listen. These days, the only people who still listen are the ones who were there. Everyone else sits patiently until the tale is complete, a frozen smile on their faces, trying to figure out if they should laugh at the events that transpired. Some feel too real to be funny.

Fair warning, dear reader: this story contains an unhealthy balance of horror and humor. For those who work in retail or any soul-crushing customer service experience, this story *must* be funny because otherwise we would weep over our own misfortunes. Or finally tell the customers what we truly think of them.

The following story is no longer true because it has been told to anyone who will still listen. At this point, we cannot remember when this happened, how it really happened, or to whom it happened. I have tried to compile the memories of those who were witness to the reign of Dave Bradley to create a tale that remains true to its protagonist. Dave Bradley is not this person's real name, but a culmination of customer qualities that have come together to have the same unbelievable brightness of a supernova. The celestial fragments fall to Earth and become part of the landscape. Dave Bradley is the human equivalent of space garbage.

The following story is probably true because it happens every day within the realms of customer service.

The following story is most likely two truths and a lie because Dave Bradley is both protagonist and antagonist. He is the hero and the villain. The moral at the end of a long-winded story that we have heard too many times. That last customer who shows up three minutes before closing to "just get a few things." Dave Bradley is the itchy tag on your uniform, the meager paycheck for too much work.

Dave Bradley is metaphor and hyperbole - an exaggeration hiding behind a very real truth. He is the Fool and the Truth-teller. He is also the Tower of Calamity. Dave Bradley has become such an urban legend, I cannot remember his real name. But I can still hear his slow shuffle of footsteps as he tries to get away with a lobster from the seafood tank.

We remember the old writing adage (ahem, *lie*) to "write what you know." This is terrible advice because it makes you remember people like Dave Bradley. I have learned that working in customer service is akin to standing outside in a storm wearing a suit of armor and holding a metal rod. Every day.

Customer service is listening to people's problems and putting up with people's abuses. Then, someone like Dave Bradley comes along and unites an entire store. Now, you have something worth fighting for. Or at least until you clock out at the end of your shift. Despite the capitalist deception that people subscribe to, customer service does not build character. When I went to college, I discovered a population of young adults who did not "build character" at a grocery store or retail giant.

Did you know there are other jobs for young people? I didn't.

Today, those young people are now adults who live everyday with a confidence that is unfathomable to someone who argued with a person over how many shrimps were in a frozen food bag. Because of that frozen shrimp experience, I don't eat seafood and I apologize when I bump into a chair. My "character" is built upon being afraid of loud noises, refusing to shop in a grocery store for longer than fifteen minutes, and waiting for the next horrible frozen shrimp argument. *I know it's around the corner.*

What I did find is that customer service is about understanding the basic components of the human condition: we all want to be heard and to be a part of something. Also, never get between people and their groceries. Or their right to be absolutely horrible to someone wearing a brightly colored uniform and name tag.

I also learned a few more truths along the way:

- If a customer tells you to smell spoiled meat, chances are they're telling the truth. Don't smell it; no matter how much they insist.
- If a coworker tells you to smell spoiled meat, chances are they're telling the truth *because they listened to the customer above* and now want you to feel terrible too. I still advise not smelling spoiled meat, but this will depend on your level of "empathy." (I place this in quotations because if you have empathy and continue to work in customer service, you have already lost)
- If you see an individual stuffing batteries down their pants in the diaper aisle, the chances are very good that they did not, in fact, purchase

these batteries.

- People will buy junk food and then always buy diet soda. This is a fact of life. You are not funny or special to notice this. Do not think you are dazzling your coworkers with this knowledge. You will become a pariah.
- All uniforms are terrible. Get over it. You aren't here to win *Project Runway*.
- Angry customers can smell fear. This is a scientifically proven fact.
- You're right; your boss DOES hate you.
- The people you work with are the only ones who truly understand what you are going through. They will be your guardian angels and the demons sent to torture you. You will snap at each other on the bad days and protect each other on the good days. They are your grocery store family.
- Time does not heal all wounds. These memories will stay fresh for a very long time. So long, in fact, that you will write about them. This is akin to telling someone to smell spoiled meat.
- It's okay to not laugh at dumb jokes made by customers. Similar to diet soda conversations,

they aren't funny either. Your laughter will only encourage them. Any hope you have at making friends will disappear and you will spend your fifteen minute break watching everyone else build friendships. As for you, you will drink your non-name brand cola that you purchased for fifty cents because you threw it against one of the walls in the dairy case as a way to create damaged goods and only pay fifty cents.

• While the damaged goods hack is true, don't repeat that.

• Seriously, don't repeat it. I think I can still get in trouble for it, twenty years later.

• You're still thinking of repeating it? *Because it's so funny no one will believe it?* Well: they will believe it. And I will get into trouble. You will be labeled a snitch. A snitch who laughs at customer's bad jokes and drinks broken soda.

• You did this to yourself.

The following story, which is partially true, no longer true, mostly true, and probably still true, is dedicated to all the supermarket employees and their Dave Bradleys.

I hear you and I understand.

Or at least until my shift is over. Then you're on your own.

The Legend of
Dave Bradley

People come into your life for a reason. Someone told me that once, or maybe it was on an embroidered pillow.

People come into your life for a reason. An embroidered pillow taught me that.

Sometimes these particular people arrive to make you a better person or to teach you something you didn't know about yourself. I am not here to argue the existence of this mysterious group of earth angels. There are people like that.

And then, there are people like Dave Bradley.

Living in a beach town, the only reasonable, respectable source of income for a teenager, if you weren't cleaning the houses of the rich families who traveled from North Jersey or New York to stay the summer, is to work at the local supermarket. We were the last supermarket on the strip of highway before Long Beach Island. This meant we were busy in the summer and bored in the winter.

My first day at the Jersey Shop N'Bag, I was a nervous fourteen-year-old in an oversized white shirt. The white shirt was meant to expose the newbies for the frauds they were - teenagers who needed the money and who never had a previous job. Luckily, this poor beach town created other nervous "white shirts," and we formed a support group of Shop N'Bag teenagers who never went to the beach in the summer, who cleaned houses in the daytime and rang up groceries in the evening. Truth be told, we desperately wanted to be like our summer vacationing counterparts, but we were born in the lower end of the socio-economic spectrum. Therefore, while our peers luxuriated on the (questionably clean) beaches of South Jersey and treated themselves to boardwalk frivolities, we nursed our paper cuts brought on by the brown bags we filled with groceries and cooled ourselves off from the summer heat by sticking our heads in the frozen food cases. Our minimum wage paychecks meant another semester of college or a chance to fix those old cars that we bought from (questionably clean) car lots along Route 37.

In terms of character-building experiences, we were storefront warriors. We knew we didn't have it all, but we had each other. In fact, it was only when I went away to college did I realize that some teenagers have very different summer experiences. Very different. Meaning, they had the choice to see their families (although they mostly chose not to) in summer homes or trips to Europe rather than passing them in the hallway on the way to the bathroom to get ready for work. In our families, everyone was at work. To our mothers, they were grateful to places like the Jersey Shop N'Bag because summer jobs kept us busy and out of trouble. Being able to "pick up a few things" after your grocery shift also meant that one item was taken off their very crowded plates.

To make up for working double shifts and missing family dinners or weekend events, we leaned on each other in ways that could be considered both endearing and codependent.

In my fondest memories, working at the Jersey Shop N'Bag was akin to working with family. I'm not kidding - there were families that actually all worked together. Parents usually maintained a respectful distance in different departments, siblings worked together on the Front End, and local teachers, mentors, and neighbors stopped by to pick up a few items before heading home from work. To make up for the fact that some of us didn't see their families much during the busy summers, those parents would take a lot of us under their wings. They made sure we took our breaks, had enough water, and had enough to eat. They would counsel us over heartbreaks or friend dramas. Some of us needed that stability and some of us just needed company. I had found my people at an age when I desperately needed to be a part of something bigger than myself.

In my most brutal memories, working at the Jersey Shop N'Bag was akin to watching my optimistic youth die, as we gathered around a formica table, dipping pieces of hot Italian bread into jars of salad dressing. Yes, we survived the summer rush, the lean winter times, and came out alive during the biannual "Stock N'Bag" sale where most canned goods and bottles were a quarter apiece. To this day, I believe the dark depths of hell is a "Stock N'Bag" sale right before a hurricane on Long Beach Island. I also believe Dante would agree with me. Or not. He strikes me as the type of person who would be in the vacation homes rather than cleaning or filling them with food.

Over time, I graduated from the literal bottom of the Front End, bagging groceries as they traveled down the moving belt of the register (at a speed no human should compete with) and onto their journey into the paper-plastic combination that always seems to delight the blue-haired old ladies, and I sailed into the Front End as a cashier. From there, I turned my unsatiated ambition to the Courtesy Desk at the front of the entrance. You were the first face the customer would see as they entered the brightly-lit carnival of Produce, Grocery, NonFoods, Health & Beauty Aids (HABA to the layman), and Frozen Foods. You were the last face the Front End would see as they handed in their cashier tills to be counted and walked out of the store, wounded and broken from a day of hauling kitty litter and lemons (BUT NOT IN THE SAME

BAG, as the blue-hairs would screech; they were unaware that we were subjected to bagging how-to videos every six months and we placed said items into same bag for no other reason than we hated you, the customer, in that particular moment).

The Courtesy Desk fulfilled my thirst for power and elitism in a small pond, as we all believed that we were in charge of the store. This is entirely untrue, as they were various levels of corporate hierarchy, but this small taste of power is enough for any eighteen-year-old. It also goes to show that as an eighteen-year-old, my youthful hubris kept me from truly understanding how the world works. To me, the Jersey Shop N'Bag was my ecosystem - it had numerous food and water sources, healthy competition between departments, infighting within these departments, and complicated interpersonal relationships, a natural causality when you put young people together for an extended period of time. Before we had the *Real Housewives* franchise, we had the delicious dramatic relationship tension that began in Produce and ended somewhere next to the Hot Pockets.

As we know from all fairy tales, action/adventure films, and superhero stories, this type of power comes with a price. The bright-eyed optimism fades pretty quickly - usually after your first summer season - and you take on the personality of that troll that bothered the Billy Goats Gruff. Screw those Billy Goats Gruff who want something better. You have become the petty drama and it suits you just fine.

In fact, it fits as snugly as the new brightly colored polyester-blend shirt that signifies you've been here way too long. Suddenly, you don't want any trouble - just to cower in the comforting darkness under your bridge, dipping pieces of hot Italian bread into jars of salad dressing.

****

As with any monotonous customer service job, the drama and the paltry pay slowly recede into the background and you find yourself going through the motions. Of course, something strange happens at least once a day - we do work with the public, after all. But it all becomes part of the buzzing background noise that plays overhead, a horrifying lullaby that never ends.

It is a truth universally acknowledged that retail

music is designed to break the spirit of any customer service employee. This is done through syncopated rhythms that remind us we "only have tonight" or "tonight is the night" for "us/anything/dreams/the moment/true love." These songs are played on loop as the doomed customer service employee realizes that they *do not* have tonight, but instead an everlasting shift of repetitive physical labor. To have tonight or true love or dreams of any caliber, one must also have the energy to pursue these things. After working a double shift or all weekend, the best you can do is watch a reality TV marathon pretending you hate everyone on the screen, but secretly glad that you aren't dealing with this in real time because today is your day off. But wait…is that your phone ringing? Oh no, it's the manager. They're calling because someone called out - they know it's your day off, but can you come in? *No pressure*, they say with a voice that makes it very clear that there is pressure and you need to say yes because it wasn't a request, but they need to make it sound this way for legal purposes. You keep one eye on the frozen frame of the TV - someone is about to get bitch-slapped and you really want to know how it ends (you know how it ends.

Someone just bitch-slapped your day off). But it isn't meant to be. Instead, you tell them you will be right there, put on that polyester-blend shirt and leave the TV as it was - a frozen horror show of rich people living their lives. Because they only have tonight. You, on the other hand, have six hours before your chance at tonight. However, that frozen frame - the one that will startle your family when they come home, also exhausted from work - that, my friend, is proof that YOU WERE HERE.

Aside from the overly optimistic tunes, there is the darkest, most hope-crushing retail music of all. The one that begins with a piano intro, then slowly picks up speed or slows down, depending on the maestro's demands. The plush-pop sound spills through the speakers, filling every molecule of air within the air-conditioned walls of the supermarket with earworms that will take up residence and alter the gray matter of your brain. These notes will haunt you well into adulthood.

The piano picks up speed, becoming the essence of every individual who enters. The music is overwhelming, filled with longing, the need to seek one's own space in the world. The musician is insistent now: *you are here for a double shift. You have no choice but to listen.* The piano mocks you, reminding you of the Sisyphean tasks that await through life's demands:

Movin' out.

Starting the fire.

Playing us a song.

What was that? I'm describing Billy Joel's musical catalog? Right. Let me try again:

The monotony of customer service is a Billy Joel song (author's note: I have no problem with Billy Joel. He seems okay to me. However, I really think Mr. Joel should discuss where his catalog ends up - does he know his songs are playing on loop in grocery stores? Does he know that the lobsters in the seafood tanks are trained to respond to his music? Does he know that the teenagers who work there are using them as anthems to save up and leave this town? One of our cashiers, named Anthony, heard a specific Billy Joel song, was convinced that Billy Joel was speaking to him, and quit on the spot. You know which song I'm talking about. Mr. Billy Joel, you did that.)

Anyway, like all customer service positions, eventually the nervousness and fear of not doing well fades away and you begin each day thinking hopefully to yourself, "Maybe *this* is the day I get fired." Granted, that would cause more trouble further down the line, BUUUUUT you would get at least one evening off. Particularly in the summer, our shifts were long - mainly because people would call out sick and we would already be there, so why not? Why not call home and say that you are taking on another few hours? Why not scrape together what little hourly pay there was?

Why not take your break hiding in the bread aisle, letting the delicious aromas lull you into a calming, yet false, tranquil state?

Why not sneak away and place bets on which lobster will escape that day? (Pro tip: the one no one suspects. Another pro tip: try not to pick a dead one).

Why not call the Seafood Department and scream, "Got any crabs?!" when they pick up the phone?

Why not forget that the phone is connected to the rest of the store and not only has the manager heard you, but the Seafood Department knows where you are because your department number lit up on the phone when they answered?

Why not pet that adorable puppy that the customer has brought into a food store?

Why not walk away from the adorable puppy and then make the announcement over the loudspeaker: "Attention, customers, we want to remind you that *only service animals* are allowed in the store?"

Why not buy a package of mini cupcakes and eat them over a trash can in the breakroom, telling yourself that *this is the last time?*

Again, I ask you: *Por que não?*

****

Of course, it wasn't always so ordinary. For the seven years I worked at Jersey Shop N'Bag, we were subjected to the experience that was Dave Bradley. Dave Bradley's name is so well known that speaking the two words aloud will result in anyone contributing their favorite Bradley moment even to this day. Most were true at some time, but now the stories have been strained and stretched, pulled into the brink of magnification, enhancing a person who now resembles caricature more than character. But fact and fiction have become muddled throughout the years and my almost-middle aged sensibilities have complicated the memories further.

So this story has developed the way Dave Bradley lived: complicated, inconsistent, and walking with a limp due to the amount of stolen material stuffed into its pants.

Dave Bradley was a bad case of herpes.

(Please note here: Dave Bradley wasn't "like" a bad case of herpes. That would indicate a comparison, which this is not. In order for a simile to work, the two ideas being compared must come together to form a vivid description. Dave Bradley was already vivid and mostly awful, so I'm going to stick with my original assessment.

One day I will look back and determine that Dave Bradley was a fever dream manifested by all of us due to some environmental issue. But for now, he is herpes.)

Just when you thought you were living your life carefree, Dave Bradley would show up at the most inconvenient time and completely ruin your day. The only way to get rid of Dave Bradley was to wait it out. And then pray he would never return, which he always did. But, unlike herpes, you can't cure a case of Dave Bradley with drugs. On the contrary: he had used so many drugs in his high school "career" that he had developed a tolerance that is still considered a scientific miracle today. Since I didn't have the privilege of attending the same high school as Dave

Bradley, most of my encounters with him centered around his visits to the Jersey Shop N'Bag.

The first day I met Dave Bradley, his pale, gangly frame slouched against the Courtesy Desk as he leaned forward to tell me there wasn't any toilet paper left in the ladies' room. His clothes were drenched with sweat and he smelled very strongly of cheap bourbon and wine coolers, a little odd for a Tuesday morning, but I nodded at his statement and sent him on his way. An hour later, he was led out by the local police for trying to drink the water in the lobster tank. He insisted the lobsters did not survive the dinosaur asteroid in order to be captured and eaten by the human equivalent of dinosaurs. To the credit of the local police, they didn't ask what the human equivalent of dinosaurs would actually be, and I always wondered if we perhaps missed an opportunity to learn something from Dave Bradley. Chris in Seafood insisted the lobsters had been traumatized by the ordeal, but we knew she was riding out the Dave Bradley experience high. To have Dave Bradley make a scene in your department made you a celebrity for a few weeks. Everyone wanted to hear your story. If you had a day off the day it happened, the amount of shame you carried with you lasted until his next visit. Granted, this happened in a matter of months, but what if he chose someone else? Another department?

What if you missed *your* chance?

Chris and the rest of the people in Seafood never experienced another Dave Bradley encounter because he set his sights on Lottery next.

In a few months, Dave Bradley came back to buy lottery tickets. He tried to pay with Monopoly money and a bottle cap. When the Lottery attendant refused, he offered her anything that was in his wallet, except for the coupon for a full bikini wax. That particular item he took out and tucked it safely away in his back pocket.

"Absolutely not," the lottery attendant said.

"What?! But this bottle cap looks like a Pog!" Dave Bradley insisted.

"What's a Pog?" the lottery attendant asked. (I swear, kids these days!)

"It's like a bottle cap," Dave Bradley said.

When she refused again to box his Pick 3 numbers, he knocked over the entire display of *Shrek* DVDs and had to be escorted out by the police.

The third time the police were dispatched on

account of Dave Bradley, he wasn't even in the store. He had arrived early to drop his wheelchair bound mother near the Produce section. She was a sweet woman who suffered from age-related macular degeneration and a bad hip. We enjoyed Mrs. Bradley because she would often stay in the Produce section smiling to herself and singing along to the music overhead. Unfortunately, on this day, her good humor ran out after three hours when Dave Bradley didn't return. She called over one of the Produce employees.

"Excuse me, young man?" called Mrs. Bradley.

Immediately, Matthew rushed over to her. "What can I help you with, Mrs. Bradley?" he asked.

"Would you be a dear and call my son please?" Mrs. Bradley said.

"Is he coming to pick you up?" (Oh, Matthew, how naive!)

"Yes, dear. After he finishes his drop-off. Can you call his cell phone please?"

As Matthew wheeled Mrs. Bradley toward the phones, he committed a cardinal sin: he asked follow-up questions (sweet, naive Matthew!). Through his questions, he discovered that 1) Mrs. Bradley was cold in Produce and preferred lobster-watching in

Seafood, 2) Dave Bradley was probably selling drugs, and 3) Mrs. Bradley was going to miss her stories on TV soon and this would transform her into a horrible, nasty person.

Matthew wheeled Mrs. Bradley around the store for three hours. In a narrative sleight of hand worthy of an Oracle, Mrs. Bradley *did* miss her stories and she *did* transform into a horrible, nasty person. Matthew accompanied her from department to department in a desperate attempt for likeability, a need to be loved despite his polyester-blend shirt proclaiming that this was, in fact, truly impossible.

Three hours and 26 items later, Mrs. Bradley was picked up by another family member.

Three hours and 40 minutes later, Matthew was still putting away the 26 items.

Three hours and 56 minutes later, 14 of the items, which were bags of frozen broccoli, didn't make it and had to be sent to "go backs," the purgatory for all food items. Fourteen bags of frozen broccoli never returned to the shelves. They say that broccoli was trashed and the grocery manager wept over the lost earnings. But that may be just a rumor.

They say Matthew never helped a customer after

that. But that may be just another rumor.

Once the initial shock of meeting Dave Bradley wore off, we didn't pay much attention to Dave Bradley's antics. They may have been irritating, but it gave the bored Shop N'Bag workers something to laugh at. We silently appreciated his company and would even fight over who got to hit the police department on speed dial.

Dave Bradley was a democratizing force at the Jersey shore. While our rich teenage counterparts were lying on the beach and coming into the store in their bathing suits for more suntan lotion and snacks, we were able to look them in the eye and know we were having a better summer than them. Dave Bradley was our "movies on the beach" or walk along the boardwalk. We were young and witnessing a revolution in what it means to be free and Dave Bradley was that icon of freedom to us: he didn't have a real job that we knew of and we weren't sure where he lived or where he actually came from. Some believe it's similar to Batman and the Joker. One day the Shop N'Bag was built and the next day, Dave Bradley showed up. Others claimed that, like Jimmie Leeds, he had always been around. And still some others believe Dave Bradley *was* Jimmie Leeds.

When Dave Bradley was sent away to County for harassing people in the Wal-Mart parking lot, Jersey Shop N'Bag lost a little piece of itself. We tried not to let it get to us, but we did feel a bit cheated. The lobster tank was good enough to terrorize and building a fort out of the rye bread display was fine for a Saturday, but Dave Bradley chose another store as his source of real trouble. What - we weren't good enough for an actual crime? Were we (I shiver to think of it even now) *the other store?*

To quote the last police officer that escorted Dave Bradley out of the store, "You can all go back to work now." So we did.

Soon we stopped keeping an eye on the front door. We entertained ourselves with the more eccentric customers, who were still weird but very much law-abiding. Most importantly, we stuck together in our hour of disappointment. Our proverbial father figure went out for a pack of smokes and never returned - we were our own family now.

As with some things, you find a way to fill the petty void. One summer we created an Ultimate

Frisbee team but lost most of the Frisbees in the cranberry bogs, which ended with infighting.

The winter of that year, they told us there would be no food in the back room (this truly doesn't matter in the grand scheme of things, but I'm still mad about it). At first we thought it meant big platters from the deli - you know the ones with all the delicious things - but they meant all the food. No food at all! But I digress (for now).

Another summer we all tried to form a cooking club, but there were too many allergies, so it ended with infighting.

The winter of that year, Steffy broke up with her long-time boyfriend (they had been together since the sixth grade), then got him back, then broke up with him again, then got him back, then broke up with him again, then got him back...this also ended with infighting - we just weren't sure which side we were on.

The following takes place over three days.

Or maybe it was one day.

Or possibly a week.

We had a lot going on.

After a dry summer, followed by a harsh winter, and peppered with cabin-fevered grocery store infighting, the return of Dave Bradley was entirely unexpected. He padded in barefoot, gave the Courtesy Desk a nod, and headed straight for the hair dye. "Oh my sweet Lord," Benny breathed. He leaned over the counter to get a better look, his six-foot-three frame knocking over the lower cigarette shelf behind him. Three packs of Viceroys spilled out under his feet. "Is that who I think it is?"

I followed his gaze. My heart leapt into my throat. *Papa? Is that you? Have you returned to us?*

"It's Dave Bradley alright." My voice was even - I couldn't give away any hope. Our entire summer experience - a summer of joyful stress-eating, combined with arguing over absolutely nothing but entirely something - was now in the grimy hands of one Dave Bradley.

"Why is he going for the hair dye?" Benny asked suddenly. "What, he doesn't come in for a year and stops in to change his hair color to avoid arrest?" This was Benny's way - to push away those closest to him in fear of being hurt again.

"Benny," Em said. Now she was leaning over the

counter, peering into the aisles. She was the nicest of the Courtesy crew, always apologizing for Benny's harsh words or Char's insults. Em had just received her orange shirt two months ago, finally making her one of us. Em had a heart about her, one that will erode slowly over the coming years, but for now she was how we all once were- full of hope and of promise for what Dave Bradley might bring. "Maybe Dave Bradley didn't come in here for hair dye. Maybe he's changed."

Benny scoffed and went back to counting tills. But it turns out Em was right: He *had* changed. No more pestering employees and trying to free lobsters. Dave Bradley didn't come in to change his hair color.

He came in to steal batteries. He ended up shoving ten packs of batteries down his pants. He would have gotten away with it if one of the store managers didn't catch him. When Dave Bradley started running toward the exit, a package of AAAs fell out of a pant leg. He ended up slipping on it and hitting his head on the trash can. Not the comeback we were expecting, but it takes time to get back into the rhythm.

Before long, Jersey Shop N'Bag was hit with a lawsuit, or so the story goes. We didn't see any paperwork, but the parents in the other departments swore this is what brought on the next series of events. Apparently, Dave Bradley felt the trash cans were a serious hazard and their placement in the store - next to the entrance and exit, away from all incoming foot traffic - needed to be reconsidered. It should go without saying that the courts disagreed with Dave Bradley's plan "to remove all trash cans in the world." He didn't go back to county jail; they just told him never to set foot in the store ever again, to seek professional counseling, and to pay for the damage to the trash can.

Dave Bradley responded to these requests by standing outside the store playing old folk songs on his guitar. When one of the store managers approached him, Dave Bradley would explain calmly that he found Jesus and wanted to share his gift of music to the world. It was fortunate for Dave Bradley that Jesus found him because none of the churches in the area wanted to claim Dave Bradley as a congregant. However, it was unfortunate for Dave Bradley that he found a guitar without any strings. He would sit outside the store, barefoot and making guitar sound effects as he strummed. Some kinder souls would throw a few pennies his way. Dave Bradley would take this as a personal affront - who were they to chuck pennies at him?- and verbally attack them as they pushed their carts to their cars. Eventually he traded his guitar for more wine coolers and gave them to the young kids who pushed the carts back into the "Cart Corral." In time, the cart boys were fired for possessing alcohol. In truth, they were only wine coolers. In short, we were all embarrassed for them. In all, the stakes had been raised.

Dave Bradley had officially become an agent of chaos. It's funny how perceptions change from white shirt to polyester-blend orange shirt. In my youth, we saw Dave Bradley as equal parts entertainment and equal parts revolutionary. Here was a guy that rejected society's expectations of teenagers like us - we worked and worked but for what? For customers to yell at us? For customers to assume that we were stupid or had made bad life choices? For money that was never enough? To ring up name brand goods while we pinched pennies *in the grocery store where we worked* to buy the cheaper version? Yet here was Dave Bradley, swimming with the lobsters (sort of) and taking on Big Trash Can (sort of).

Unfortunately with age and experience comes the polyester-blend shirt. In the time that it took for Dave Bradley to return to us - ruining battery displays, passing out wine coolers, not playing the guitar - we have all aged out of Dave Bradley's nonsense. Now he was nothing more than an annoyance and more paperwork to fill out every time he committed another misdemeanor. There may have been two reasons for this:

1. Like all great performers, Dave Bradley was running out of new material. Or maybe he was losing his passion for the role. Sure, it was fun to watch him fight the inflatable skydancer that stood outside the Jersey Shop N'Bag, but you can see his heart wasn't in it. These days, it's all about flash to get the likes and Dave Bradley only knew the classics. He began his reign at a different time, and - oh hold on, he's *really* fighting that skydancer. We'll finish this later.

2. Most of the Courtesy Desk went off to college and our Shop N'Bag stories

were limited to our returns for winter and summer breaks. Suddenly, the sheen that comes with having a grocery store family was being replaced with real world issues, adult decisions, and new people and places. To have Dave Bradley return time and time again, for the same stupid reasons, made us resent the entire situation. If I had to be honest (and I don't want to), I was so angry and frustrated with myself. Why couldn't I figure out my life? What was I supposed to do after college? To see Dave Bradley stuck in a loop also made me feel that I was doomed to the same fate. Being angry at Dave Bradley that summer allowed me to push aside any adult decisions that needed to be made. It didn't make me feel better to ignore them, but at least I could blame Dave Bradley for diverting my attention to him rather than blame myself.

And so, Dave Bradley became a phantom told by older Shop N'Bag workers. The white shirts would sit in the teal colored break room, wide-eyed and eager to hear the end of the Dave Bradley story. "Then what did he do?" "Then what did you do?" They would ask their questions, leaning forward in nervous anticipation that only lives in the early years of customer service experience. They wanted to be prepared for their own unruly customer experiences, but they weren't getting the full teachings. We didn't tell the stories with the same fervor as we used to. We told them in a matter-of-fact way, the same way you would recite any memorized fact. Dave Bradley's chaotic presence became summarized which in turn made him lose his appeal. Never meet your heroes, kids.

As veterans, and almost-adults, our job was to provide a moral to the Dave Bradley tale - stay in school, don't fight with trash cans, always take care of your mother. But there was one major problem with our story - the thread we didn't want to pull in fear of losing all Shop N'Bag credibility: there wasn't an ending. As quickly as he returned and as quickly as it took to finish off those shitty wine coolers, Dave Bradley simply disappeared. I felt his absence the way I did when my tonsils were removed. It wasn't a huge change to have them gone, but still I knew they had once been there. Sometimes when reading the newspaper, I would come across a headline: "Local Man Charged with Drugs" or "Local Man Harasses Sheep" and my heart would skip. I would quickly scan the article, wondering if I'd see that name in black and white.

That didn't happen. Dave Bradley really did take a break from us. What I didn't know at the time was Dave Bradley's grand finale would remind me of why I stayed so long at the Jersey Shop N'Bag.

****

Going on my seventh year at the Jersey Shop N'Bag, I decided to call it quits. The pay was bad, the hours were horrible and the 15-year-old cart boys catcalling me began to affect my work performance. But little did I know that my last few weeks at Shop N'Bag would involve a Dave Bradley story that would make Homer jealous (it took Odysseus twenty years to get home - ha! Try working a full holiday weekend shift).

Similar to the beginning of a horror movie, it started out as a typical work day. Char and I were in the back office counting out the afternoon registers and arguing over the boombox that we had all pitched in and bought on sale at Target the week before. We wanted to leave the next Courtesy Desk with a gift to remember us by, while ignoring the reality that most people were now listening to iPods and current music of the early 2000s. We saw this gesture as selfless and heroic, without realizing that we were now the boring weird old-timers who were frightening and bumming out the newest, and youngest, employees. As far as we were concerned, this boombox was our legacy, as were the CDs we got in the bargain bin on the end cap by the shampoo aisle. You can never have enough *Celtic Woman* CDs. This is a fact.

Being the veterans that we were, the Courtesy crew and I had settled into our usual routine. Char and I would close out the back office and Benny and Em would work the front. On this particular week, Benny was off on a cruise, leaving the three of us to hold down the counter. We worked in comfortable silence, the kind that can only be earned after many years together on the job. We were about halfway through *Celtic Woman* when Char made an announcement:

"I found someone to help me get over Brandon,"

she said this between songs which shows what a wonderful person she truly is.

"Really?" I asked. Char and Brandon had dated for three years, but Brandon had broken up with her at the beginning of the summer because he wanted to pursue his dream of being in a band. To this day, Brandon still hasn't found people who want to be in a band and has still not learned how to write or play any form of music.

"Yeah, his name is Will and he works in NonFoods," Char started to fill out a deposit slip, being very careful not to make eye contact.

"Which one is he?" I asked.

"The one who looks like he has caterpillars for eyebrows."

"Wait, you want to hook up with someone who has caterpillars for eyebrows?"

"Ew, Amanda," Char said, "They aren't real caterpillars. But I do need you to help me."

"What do you want me to do?" I asked, making sure to promise nothing until I hear the entire plan. Usually helping Char requires looking up the chosen boy's Loyalty Card account on the computer and then accompanying her to his house for some late-night drive-by. As illegal as most of her requests were, they were always doable. Since this breakup, Char was desperate to show off a boyfriend who wasn't in a band and her requests were getting weirder and more insistent. A prospect more caterpillar than boy was a new one.

"Go on a double date with us." Char suddenly turned away, concentrating hard on counting her stack of money. Without looking at me, she continued, "His friend likes you."

That didn't sound too bad. "Alright," I said, grateful it was something that didn't involve committing some sort of crime. "Who's his friend?"

"He actually works here too. Theo from the Front End."

I almost dropped the money I was counting. "Char, Theo is sixteen."

"And Will is seventeen."

"Char, we're twenty-one years old. They don't even have their driver's licenses!"

"So? We do!" Char said.

"And by law, Theo has to be in by 10pm on weeknights," I finished.

"I'm still not getting it," she said.

"Then get this: I'm not doing it. It's gross."

"Amanda," Char said. "Why are you being so selfish? I'm not asking you to marry him. And even if I did, you should say yes because you're my best friend."

"I could go to jail!" I exclaimed.

"No, you can't. I already looked it up. Don't you think he's cute?"

"No, because he hasn't even hit puberty yet," I said. "Get my sister to go out with him. She's eighteen."

"Um, I really don't want to spend my night with minors," Char said. "What do you think I'm some sort of freak?"

Before I could reply in a way that was both funny and hurtful, we were interrupted by someone yelling out front. "Um, a little help?" came Em's timid voice from the front counter.

"Yes!" I shouted a bit too loudly, grateful for the interruption.

"This isn't over," Char hissed at me, much like a villain in a Bond film. Then, Char turned to the window facing the counter. "Oh my God," she said in a flat tone. I looked over at her face. I've only seen this look of horror on Char's face twice in the entire five years we've been friends: when Billy Joel got into his car accident and when we found out Brandon was dating the girl who won first place in our high school talent show by putting her body through a wire hanger (the second place winner was the kid who accidentally brought in a live dove for a magic show and it flew into the stage lights. RIP). I followed her gaze out front.

Standing in front of Em and screaming at the top of his lungs was Dave Bradley. He looked thinner, but showered, and slightly older. True to form, he was still wearing board shorts and a band T-shirt from the 90's. He waved his arms wildly and the vein in his neck pulsed at an unnatural rate. Char and I made our way out front.

"I demand to speak with a manager!" Dave Bradley yelled. "This is an injustice! It's discrimination!"

Em watched this display of human sadness evenly. We could see the last pieces of her "white shirt" humanity dissolve and the cold, customer service retail shell of the Courtesy Desk begin to form around her soul. The transformation was finally complete. "Discrimination of what, asshole?" Em muttered under her breath. Louder she said, "What's the problem, Dave?"

"Oh no, I'm not telling you. Get me a manager," Dave Bradley drummed his fingers on the counter and glared at us. "I have all the time in the world."

"That's because you're a deadbeat, Bradley," Char snapped.

"Shut the hell up, Char," he retorted. "You don't know me."

"Okay," Char said. "Everyone who is allowed within three feet of the lobster tank, raise your hands."

Em, Char and I raised our hands and we glanced over at Dave Bradley. Dave Bradley's face turned purple. "Get me a manager!" he demanded. "I'll fucking have your jobs."

"Bradley," Char said. "You can't; they perform random drug tests."

"And you have to show up every day," I added helpfully.

Dave Bradley was about to retort, but then considered it. "Well, this job is dumb anyway," he finally said. He was right, of course, but we wouldn't give him the satisfaction.

I sighed, officially done with this conversation

and whatever Bradley had up his sleeve. "Bradley, I'll get you a manager. Just stop talking for five seconds."

Dave Bradley shot me a smug smile and turned his back to us. Char threw a book of matches at him, missed, and watched it sail over his shoulder. Dave Bradley didn't even notice. A few minutes later the manager on duty, Mr. C., walked up to the counter. He walked with the briskness and purpose of a manager who was going to make a difference today, who was going to show his town how well he can handle customer complaints.

Mr. C. was walking toward us with his "let's help a customer today!" smile. Unfortunately, Mr. C. didn't see what was waiting for him right away. His customer service smile quickly disappeared when he noticed Dave Bradley. "What is it, Mr. Bradley?" Mr. C. asked.

"Listen, man, I have a situation with your store," Dave Bradley said. "During the blizzard I slipped on the ice and I hurt my ankle. I need to fill out an accident report."

Mr. C. suddenly looked more tired. "Dave, it's July."

"It happened in the winter *obviously*. And now my ankle is acting up." Dave Bradley pointed to his left ankle, thought better of it, and switched to the right one.

"It's too late," Mr. C. said. "Look, if you came in when it happened, we could have done something about it. But we can't now."

"I couldn't come in because I wasn't allowed in your store!" Dave Bradley yelled. "How is that my fault?"

"Actually, you're still not supposed to be in here," Mr. C. informed him. "You have one chance to leave before we call the police."

Char headed over to the phone and held her finger poised over the button marked "Police." Dave Bradley was silent for a moment. Then he turned and limped out of the store, alternating between legs because he couldn't remember which one was supposed to hurt.

"Good one, Mr. C.," Char said.

"Thanks, Char." Mr. C. started to walk away. "Get back to work, folks."

We all breathed a collective sigh as whatever was starting to boil to the surface returned to the regular simmer of customers shopping for groceries. Mr. C. walked away with the confidence of a manager who has seen it and handled it all, and as a result, is expected to fix every ridiculous problem without the benefits of higher pay or recognition. Em, Char, and I watched as, in a matter of moments, Mr. C signed for a grocery delivery, helped a customer find the cereal aisle, and broke up a fight among the citizens of the "Cart Corral." (I know what you are thinking, dear reader, Dave Bradley gave up way too easily. Mr. C. was a fool).

I couldn't marvel at Mr. C.'s superpowers for too long as Will and Theo were talking towards us. They were going on break and brought enough juice boxes to share with all of us.

Ignoring Char's pleading look, I did something I thought I would never do at the Jersey Shop N'Bag: I voluntarily went back to work.

****

"So you don't want to go out with Theo?" Char asked. "Are you sure?" It was the day after Dave Bradley's strange comeback and, while the rest of us were trying to process this new information, Char was still determined to achieve her goal of dating Will.

"I'm pretty sure," I said. "I'm not in the mood to baby-sit."

"He has a pool," Char offered.

"So do you."

"Yeah, but now you can't use it because you won't help me."

Em came into the back room. "Um, I hate to interrupt this creepy, unethical conversation, but Dave Bradley is back. I think you should come out here and see this."

Char pushed past me to follow Em. "We have more to discuss," she said to me.

"Like my babysitting rate?" I asked. "You couldn't afford me."

Together, the three of us stood behind the Courtesy counter. We watched in sick fascination as Dave Bradley tried to maneuver his way into the store with crutches. They were too small for his tall frame; the air cast around his ankle was even smaller.

"It looks like the cast he had when he was twelve," Em said.

"Why did he have a cast?" I asked.

"He fell out of a tree trying to rob someone's house," Char said.

"Char, that never happened. He broke his ankle snowboarding," Em said.

"Eh, my story is better," Char said.

By now Dave Bradley had made his way to the counter. "I almost thought I wouldn't make it, ladies," he said.

"We applaud your perseverance," I said.

"What did you call me?" he asked.

"Why are you here, Bradley?" I asked. "You aren't allowed in the store."

Ignoring my last comment, Dave Bradley said coolly, "I want one of those motorized cart things that I see people using."

At first I thought he was kidding. "You're kidding," I said.

"Do I look like I'm kidding?" Dave Bradley asked. He started to tip to the side on his crutches. His arms flailed briefly before he steadied himself. "And can you hurry? My ankle really hurts."

I really didn't know what Dave Bradley was trying to accomplish. Out of all of his stunts, this was the most ridiculous - what was his endgame here? Why can't he keep his balance on those crutches? Why is Theo waving at the Courtesy Desk? To this day, I still cannot answer these questions.

I could have told him to leave. I could have called Mr. C. to the Courtesy Desk. I could have called the police. I could have let Char loose and watch her beat Dave Bradley with his own crutches (which would have been glorious). But I didn't do any of those things. What I did do was call for the motorized cart. While we waited for it, the three of us stared silently at Dave Bradley. He looked back at us innocently. I realized at that moment that I had exactly three weeks left at Shop N'Bag. Technically this would probably be the last major story I would have to tell. It made me sad in a way; a part of my life was ending. I was slowly closing the door of my first job I've ever had behind me. And the last image I would see would be Dave Bradley and these stupid crutches.

One of the cashiers, Linda, zoomed up to the Courtesy Desk in the motorized cart. When she saw Dave Bradley standing there smiling at her, her "can-do" customer service attitude vanished and she quickly jumped up from the cart to run back to the Front End. Dave Bradley watched her go. "Damn that girl is fine," he said. "How old do you think she is?"

"Sixty-three," Char answered.

"Good to know, good to know," Dave Bradley said. "Is she single?"

"No," I answered. "Linda and her husband just welcomed their third grandchild, so I think it's a long-term thing."

"Damn," Dave Bradley said. "All the good ones, right?"

He snapped out of his unrequited love for Linda and handed Em his crutches. "Hold these for me, will you?" He settled himself into the motorized cart, small cast and all, and proceeded to zoom after Linda who was quick on her feet but no match for a slowly moving cart with a determined Dave Bradley at the helm. A few seconds later we heard, "Hey, hey you, can I get your number? You know my mom right?"

I'm sure you've probably figured out by now that for the next hour and a half, we didn't get any work done. Customers came in and out, but we were too busy watching Dave Bradley try to operate his cart. He couldn't figure out how to reverse or to go forward. His attempts would result in going the wrong way and hitting a display. All the while, the lobsters watched worriedly from their tank. As much fun as it was watching Maintenance clean up the trail left by Dave Bradley, I was slowly getting annoyed. It is very distracting to count the money in the Courtesy tills to the soundtrack of screeching wheels, followed by an "ahhhhhh…dammit!" every few seconds.

Finally, Dave Bradley got the hang of it and buzzed past the Courtesy counter. "Bradley, you didn't even fill up the basket," I said. "Why are you still here?"

"You just continue counting your money and let me worry about that," he said.

"Bradley, I'm serious, I'm going to call the police," I said.

Ignoring me, Dave Bradley careened into the infamous hair dye aisle. Almost immediately, Mary, the head of security, ran to follow him. Seeing her walk toward him, Dave Bradley put the cart in reverse and headed for Bakery. He almost didn't make it when he hit the display of fresh rolls. Bags of rolls, still warm from the bakery ovens, slid to the ground and we watched in horror as the motorized cart flattened their deliciousness. It made no sound, but we watched the flattened pieces come out on the other side of the wheels. A small scream escaped me. Char crossed herself and Em put a hand over her heart. Before we could continue mourning our fallen gluten brethren, Dave Bradley bounced onto the other side of the aisle and almost ran over the representative from Make-A-Moment Greeting Cards. He gave her the thumbs-up sign and continued driving. Horrified, she followed him down the aisle and tripped over some of the bread that had spilled near her greeting cards.

About twenty minutes later, Mary called the three of us into the back room. "We have reason to believe that Mr. Bradley is stealing," she said.

Char snorted. "Shocking."

Mary ignored her and continued, "He's in aisle 3 looking at the batteries. I need someone to go in and see what he has in his cart."

"Make Amanda go," Char said. "She's from Bayonne."

"What does that have to do with anything?" I asked.

"It has to do with *everything*," Char said. "Let me know if you see Will out there."

I took the back way towards aisle 3 and walked slowly toward the humming motorized cart and the fool it was carrying. I could see Dave Bradley concentrating hard on a package of AAs. He smirked when he saw me. Store policy states that we can't accuse anyone of stealing unless we have proof. Dave Bradley knew the drill: as of right now, he was a customer. And I had to treat him as one. I looked through a few things on the shelf, keeping an eye on his cart. The monstrous steel basket in the front had a box of toothpaste, stool softeners, juice boxes and People magazine. Paid stickers were on all of them, but these looked like paid stickers from twenty years ago - not the shiny new orange stickers that proclaimed "PAID!!" proudly in Helvetica.

I was just about to report this to Mary when I heard someone behind me say, "Excuse me? miss?"

I turned to face Dave Bradley. He looked up at me. "Where's the baby powder?"

I sighed. "The next aisle over, left hand side, third shelf down."

"Thanks," he said. "I need to powder my balls."

It was at that moment that time slowed down. The store became its own world, where the outside mores of civilization no longer existed. Seven years of Shop N'Bag had finally come down to this moment - the moment that makes heroes out of the ordinary, or at least the day you earned that $10.50 an hour. The only sounds I heard were my rage pounding in my ears and the sound of the fake rain that waters the produce every twenty minutes, along with a tinny rendition of "Singin' in the Rain."

Dave Bradley and I maintained steady eye contact until the song stopped and the fake mists quieted down. Time returned and slowly, I pointed to the next aisle over. Just as slowly, Dave Bradley put his motorized cart in reverse. He hit the hair dye and I watched a few boxes fall down. He jerked forward and cruised down the aisle, making a sharp turn for the baby powder. As the zooms faded, I heard a triumphant yell from Dave Bradley: "I deserve this!" More thuds followed and I knew we lost more bread.

I feared for the lobsters.

Mary appeared beside me. "Well?" she asked.

"Items with old paid stickers," I said.

Mary's eyes lit up with a little too much glee. Given the circumstances, we can cut her a break. "Great work!" she shouted a bit too enthusiastically. She hurried after the slow-moving Dave Bradley.

I made it out of the aisle just in time to see Dave

Bradley jump out of the cart while it was still moving. He tried to run from Mary, but the cast was too small. With the cart gradually getting away from him, he fell on his face, baby powder spilling everywhere. Mary grabbed the back of his shirt and pulled him to his feet. "Come with me, please, Mr. Bradley."

Dave Bradley burst into tears. "Please don't send me back to County! I can't go back! Please don't send me back!"

Mary rolled her eyes. "Mr. Bradley, you're making a scene. You know the drill by now." She led Dave Bradley into the security office. I got into the cart and drove it up to the Courtesy Desk.

"Well?" Char asked.

"Mary got him," I said.

Char let out a happy yell and climbed over the counter. She jumped into the basket of the cart. I put the motorized cart forward and we made victory laps around the cookie display. From the Front End, we saw Linda applauding. This was her victory too.

****

Unlike the employees of Shop N'Bag, the police

63

didn't look too happy when they arrived and saw Dave Bradley sitting in the Security office. Especially when Dave Bradley caught sight of them and tried to run again, and forgot, again, that he was still wearing the small cast. "Goddammit, this kid," we heard one of the officers say as they entered the room. A few minutes later, he walked out in handcuffs. Em, Char and I waved goodbye to Dave Bradley. His eyes narrowed and he turned away.

Mary came up to the counter. "Busy day, huh?" she said.

"I can't believe he's going back to jail because he tried to steal some random things," Em said. "It's so sad."

"Oh, we didn't press charges," Mary said. "I cut him a break."

"Then why did they arrest him?" Char asked.

"There was a warrant out for Mr. Bradley's arrest. Unpaid parking tickets," Mary shrugged and headed back to her office. "So I just handed him over to the police."

After our last encounter with Dave Bradley, we were too excited to work. After we called Benny on his family cruise to brag about our adventure

("Damn! I never get to be that lucky!" he exclaimed, his words cutting out since he was on his phone in an all-inclusive resort in the Bahamas), we spent the rest of the night, counting tills and dancing to 80's pop hits until Mary called us from her office to tell us she could see us on the security cameras, and, *seriously, get back to work*. We didn't care - this was a day to celebrate. We have defeated our own fears and insecurities and have come back on the other side, ready to take on the next phase of our lives. Oh, and Dave Bradley was there too.

Alas, my victory was not meant to last because Char turned to me with that familiar glit in her eye. The one that told me this conversation would not end with our shift. "Now, about Theo," Char started to say.

I leaned over and turned up the volume. "Let's just enjoy this moment," I said. "You are too wonderful to date boys."

"But Brandon -"

"Brandon sucks," Em chimed in. "That's it. That's the end."

I nodded. "And so does his band. Whenever it happens."

"And one day Will's eyebrows will become beautiful butterflies, but not now," Em said.

We could see Char mulling this over. Deep down, I know she knew it too: we were nearing the end of an era. In a way, I think Dave Bradley sensed that we needed one more adventure and like the good fairies in *Sleeping Beauty* appeared at just the right time. He granted us one more wish - one more moment in this place to remind us that maybe, just maybe, this job did build a little character. And gave us a chosen family when we needed it most. They weren't the summers we would have chosen, but they were still significant. Who needs summer homes and European vacations when you have the Hot Foods department just a few feet away and these comfortable polyester-blend shirts? We had each other and no one had to compromise their chances in the dating pool.

After our moment of silence, punctuated by a finale that can only be done by A-ha and "Take on Me," Em was the first to speak. "This song is for Dave Bradley," she announced, raising a two thousand strap of 20's. Char raised her stapler and I raised a roll of quarters. "To Dave Bradley," we said over the music.

Our Courtesy Desk phone rang again. It was

Mary. "Seriously. *I can see you.* Put the straps of money down. Get back to work."

I wish I could tell you that we did get back to work. But Mary had to call us two more times. We tried, but we were too giddy to concentrate - there were so many possibilities in front of us! Such is the effect of a Dave Bradley encounter.

****

A full year had gone by before I returned to Jersey Shop N'Bag. On my first day of spring break, home from my new retail job (I know, I know), I stopped in to visit my sister at work. She had taken up the supermarket mantle and managed to claim a spot within the Grocery department. Like me, she knows there is a future outside of the Shop N'Bag, but also knows she still has time left. As I watched her restock the baking shelves, she said to me, "Hey, do you know Dave Bradley?"

"Kind of. Why?" I asked.

"He was in here the other day and he asked for you. I told him you didn't work here anymore and then he asked for Char or Em or Benny. I told him that they quit a few months ago too."

"What did he say?"

"Nothing. He just nodded his head and bought some soda."

"Wait…he bought something?" I couldn't believe it. That didn't sound right.

"Yeah. He had a baby with him," my sister continued. "He said he needed to get home."

I had to hold onto the shelf to steady myself. *"He kidnapped a baby?"*

My sister glanced over at me. "No, freak, it was his kid. Why would he kidnap a baby?"

At this, I had no words. It may have seemed like a weird comment to her, but it made me realize that the people that would have understood what I meant were also getting on with their lives. We were relics, those old millennials who talk about their old jobs because, frankly, it's all we know. It was a strange feeling, one that reminded me I didn't belong there anymore.

I wanted to tell her about all the things he had done in my years at the Jersey Shop N'Bag that would make it more plausible for hell to freeze over than for Dave Bradley to become a parent. I wanted to tell her all of the stories that still make Courtesy Desk veterans laugh hysterically, even though it's been told a million times and might not even be accurate anymore.

But I didn't. I just told her I'd see her at home and headed for the exit. Usually I stop to visit a cashier I had trained or knew when I worked there. Except this time, I didn't recognize anyone. We all carry that realization as heavy baggage on our backs until it finally clamors over us to look us in the eye and declare: *it's time to grow up*. It seems even Dave Bradley got the message. Maybe Dave Bradley was a good father. I wouldn't be surprised if he was; that's how it usually works out. Maybe he grew out of smoking pot all day and stealing packs of gum from convenience stores. Maybe he did those things for the same reason we were afraid to leave the Jersey Shop N'Bag: it meant accepting the world was bigger than we'd ever imagined. And we had to carve our place within it- but where do we start?. As long as we were engaged in a battle of wits with Dave Bradley, there was no reason to leave. And as long as Dave Bradley was stealing batteries, bothering Linda, and freeing lobsters, he too didn't have to grow up. We could all just exist in this strange, codependent microcosm a little longer.

To be honest, it didn't really matter if I ever saw him again: there really was no reason to. The only physical memento left of Dave Bradley, proof that he once existed, were the old pair of crutches still at the Courtesy Desk waiting to be claimed. As they wait, the features and names of the teenage employees will change and the summers will blend into one long line of faceless vacationers. Those crutches will watch the Jersey shore lose itself in Hurricane Sandy and then reclaim itself a few years later. It will last through successes and failures, changing faces and shirts. All the while, the Shop N'Bag will remain, its fluorescent sign serving as a beacon for hungry pilgrims and the teenagers paid minimum wage to serve them.

As for Dave Bradley, he will evolve into the urban legend he was destined to be, hidden within the artificial mists of the Produce section and waiting for a humble bard to tell his tale.

No Food

A Very, Very Short Epilogue About Something That
Truly Doesn't Matter In the Grand Scheme of Things
But I'm Still Mad About.

(I told you we would come back to this)

Imagine the setting: The Courtesy Booth at the Jersey Shop N'Bag. It's a soulless place, quite similar to a dystopia where authority is given to undeserving, underqualified, power-hungry individuals and the powers that be are just trying to keep the store - I mean, dystopia - alive to see another day. Now imagine a group of brave Jersey Shop N'Bag employees clustered together staring at a piece of paper pinned to the wall. There is a low hum of fear, disgust, and shock. They say nothing, but continue to stare at this piece of paper hoping it will change. Around them, people are doing their actual jobs. So much so that the working employees are bumping into the four of them who do not move from their fixation on the wall.

The sign is obvious: "No Food Is Allowed In The Back Office."

I know what you're thinking, dear reader. What does this mean? Like, no food at all? Or just big platters from the deli? This is silly - we need to have food back here. Maybe they just mean the big platters from the deli.

Read it again - maybe it says something different this time. It's obviously a prank. Or a sick joke. They probably just mean the big platters from the deli. But…what counts as a "big platter?" Maybe they mean the ones with all the food. Like turkey, roast beef, ham, salami, hummus, vegetable dip, assorted olives, lettuce.

At this point, someone jumps in, *No one eats the lettuce! It's for show!*

Our fearless heroes do not have time to work this out because the combo lock is heard on the back office door and the night manager, Mr. C, walks in. He is a kind man, but very tired. Mainly because he is the night manager in a place that has 95% of its employees under the age of twenty. Mr. C is a man in his fifties who realized too late that working with a store full of teenagers would not be fulfilling.

Mr. C. is the reason for this sign, but like we said, he is very tired. He doesn't want to argue with anyone over this. He just wants people to listen to him. Isn't that why he took this job? So that he can make a difference in the food industry and people will listen to him? Now he's stuck sneaking memos to walls and pretending that he didn't write these memos so that no one argues with him.

Did we mention that Mr. C. is very tired?

When Mr. C. is questioned about the sign, he feigns surprise *(Oh, this sign right here? That is interesting.)*. The surprise turns into confusion because now he is being asked about deli platters and he wasn't prepared for that.

Mr. C. tries to be brave
(The sign means no food. At all).

What about snacks?
No snacks.
Snacks aren't food!

What about smoothies?
No smoothies.
That's a liquid!

This is madness! Our heroes have to eat in the back room. They cannot possibly eat in the break room with everyone else! They are better than them! They control the store!

Who cares if food shouldn't be near the money tills?

Because of that *one* time? But that was one time!

How do you know it was a health code violation, Mr. C.? What are you, the health department? You know the health department?! That is so cool! Have they ever found dead rats in the store? So you think rats will come in if there's food back here? But they're dead, Mr. C., so obviously you don't have an argument here.

Mr. C. balks at this outburst. There is a moment when he tries to respond, then remembers it doesn't matter because it never matters. Nothing matters in this store. Ever.

The combo door in the back office is heard opening. Two of our heroes rush toward the sound - they know something and every moment counts. Mr. C walks in and stands at the entrance where they keep the walkie talkies. He takes one off the wall and starts trying it out. It takes Mr. C. a while to pick out one walkie talkie, despite the fact they all look the same. But it's a quiet moment and Mr. C. appreciates that. Plus he wants to take his lunch and doesn't want to talk about rats, alive or dead, anymore.

The combo is heard again and someone walks in with an armful of food. It truly is a feast. No one person would finish this amount of food in a fifteen minute break. They see Mr. C. and silently gasp in horror. They back out, trying to balance the big deli platter and the rest of the food in their arms. The door shuts quietly behind them with the rest of our heroes blocking the entrance. They are in this together.

Mr. C. looks up and sees everyone staring at him. Confused and feeling a bit awkward, he looks at them and attempts to appear authoritative (*No food in the back room, right?*). He thinks he hears a response (*Probably*) and figures it's good enough. Maybe those management books are on to something. Mr. C. picks up his chosen walkie talkie and leaves.

The combo door is heard again and not one but two of our heroes come back with armfuls of food. It is important to note that they are not helping each other with the food, but are struggling with the same amount of food. Our heroes celebrate their good fortune with a feast.

Then it all happens so fast: the combo door is heard again and Mr. C. walks back in. Our heroes have been enjoying themselves and forgot to choose a lookout. Mr. C. is faced with multiple looks of horror and food half-chewed. The apologies come quickly with pieces of food sprayed in Mr. C.'s general direction:

Mr. C. cannot comprehend the horror of what is in front of him. Think of it as the last days of Caligula but with deli platters (the big ones) and crying teenagers. Mr. C. sighs. Then he leaves. Our heroes continue to eat. A shaky truce has been created.

The next day there is a new sign in the back office. It reads, "Fine." It is unclear who put it there.

But thanks to these courageous souls, food was allowed in the back office. Until the mice came. But that story isn't mine to tell. That story, dear reader, belongs to the pest control guy.

S. Atzeni (she/they) is a writer of prose, comics, and academic scholarship. They are the co-author of *The MOTHER Principle* graphic novel series and editor of the award winning anthology series *Life in the Garden State*. Their latest book, *The Legend of Dave Bradley* was released as part of the One 'n Done series. S. Atzeni is the co-founder and editorial director of Read Furiously Publishing and currently teaches post-modernism, Holocaust studies, superheroes, and pop culture at The College of New Jersey.

Find Samantha online at:

smatzeni.com

instagram.com/smatzeni

A Note to our Furious Readers

From all of us at Read Furiously, we hope you enjoyed our latest title, *The Legend of Dave Bradley.*

There are countless narratives in this world and we would like to share as many of them as possible with our Furious Readers.

It is with this in mind that we pledge to donate a portion of these book sales to causes that are special to Read Furiously. These causes are chosen with the intent to better the lives of others who are struggling to tell their own stories.

Reading is more than a passive activity – it is the opportunity to play an active role within our world. At Read Furiously, we wish to add an active voice to the world we all share because we believe any growth within the company is aimless if we can't also nurture positive change in our local and global communities. The causes we support are culturally and socially conscious to encourage a sense of civic responsibility associated with the act of reading. Each cause has been researched thoroughly, discussed openly, and voted upon carefully by our team of Read Furiously editors.

To find out more about who, what, why, and where Read Furiously lends its support, please visit our website at readfuriously.com/charity

Happy reading and giving, Furious Readers!

Read Often, Read Well, Read Furiously!

More in the One 'n Done Series

What About Tuesday
Adam Wilson
978-0-9965227-9-3

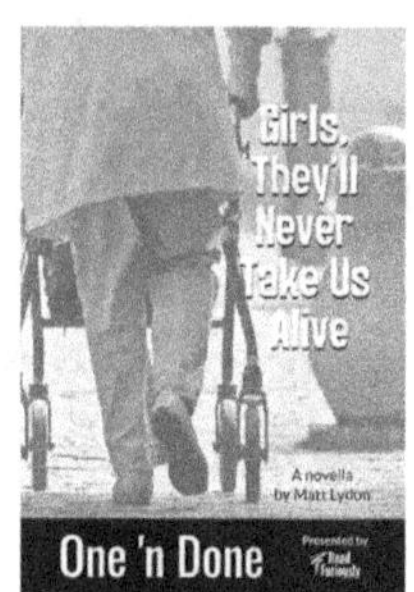

Gurls, They'll Never Take Us Alive
Matt Lydon
978-1-7337360-3-9

Brethren Hollow
Bill Hemmig
978-1-7337360-8-4

Helium
Adam Wilson
and Jeff Chin
978-1-7337360-5-3

The Legend of Dave Bradley
S Atzeni
978-1-7371758-8-9

www.ingramcontent.com/pod-product-compliance
Lightning Source LLC
Chambersburg PA
CBHW061223210726
48294CB00006B/1959